Gareth Clarke

THE EMPTY LANE

HZPublishing

Copyright © 2023 by Gareth Clarke

All rights reserved. No part of this book may be reproduced or used in any manner without written permission of the copyright owner except for the use of quotations in a book review. For more information, address: garethclarke137@gmail.com

HZPublishing

The Empty Lane

The Empty Lane

Schooldays

The Investigation

Every Day I Die

Watching

The Riverbank

The Invitation

The Coverlet

Consolation

The Empty Lane 2

The Truck Stop

Peace

Darkness

Bird of Paradise

The Darkling Sky

The Riverbank 2

The Moaning of the Pumps

The Box of Secrets

Out of True

The Turning

Perfume

Musical Box

Dust

The Empty Lane

You want to hear about the empty lane. Very well. So be it. What's there to say of an empty lane beyond that it is a lane and that it is empty. So far so good. A steady start in defining this problem. Your chin, that heavily-coated stubble, that bumptious tilt, seems to signal agreement. Very good. My mind is at peace. But, further, does the problem lie in the lane or the definition. Or within the lane. Or within the definition. Or in both. Let us say both. That this presents certain problems is indisputable, yet perhaps (why do I say perhaps) none that should prove beyond my powers to solve. Or purview. Let us say range of knowledge and understanding appropriate to the task at hand. Well-qualified. Equipped. Let us say equipment. Tools of the trade. So that is a start. That is where we set off along the empty lane, so to speak.

Shall we first define its emptiness? At once we see that the length of the lane itself presents certain difficulties. None, no doubt, that we cannot overcome. I say we. To assess, define, in some way measure the emptiness along the entire length. And then again, the kink. There is a kink. So often overlooked but vital to this attempt at definition. Let us say attempt. So at any point there is emptiness. Void. Let us say void. So that problem, the problem of emptiness, is solved more easily than I had feared. I had feared many problems involving many days, perhaps weeks of painstaking investigation, measuring, observing, photographing, all the usual techniques of forensic study. No, not forensic. This is no formal or public investigation. Merely an academic study, of purely theoretical or speculative interest. (I say merely, as if being nothing more). Yet the emptiness. I followed. Following. You brought the tools of the trade to the empty lane. We caught it at a moment in time. We captured it in its emptiness. I followed. Was following. Can't you see it yet? I watch your movements. The heavy, shuffling gait. Now swifter, eyes darting, workman's bag swinging by your side. Unseen in the empty lane. Observe, observing. The kink, the hidden section of the lane. Unseen. The dark, heavy overcoat. Sweating. Hat pulled down. The heavy beating of the drum, boom, boom, boom. So the empty lane was no longer empty.

Schooldays

School. Pleasant time, kindly playfellows. Setting the tone. Setting the standard. Marker. Marked. Marking my juvenile days. Let us say branded. Perhaps you read the words but they mean nothing. I felt nothing. There was nothing to feel. Your story, fabrication, eternal evasiveness fills me with nausea. The stench. All I ask is a straight path, without deviations. Merely clear indications relating to here or here or here. Or here. At any point the meaning is clear, the path is clearly marked. Without markers there is only confusion. Outcast from the start. Cast aside. Cast adrift. Aside. Cast, casting. Let's play catch. Who's on. Don't choose him he's weird. Look at his clothes, his socks don't match, his hair's dirty. He stinks. Stink. Rank disinhibitor. What would it take to stop their maws, their mouthing, mawkish maws. Only friends I had I made up myself. Imaginary? Yeah, imaginary. Why don't you fucking listen. Gerry was my age. He knew stuff I didn't know. Would do stuff I couldn't or wouldn't do. So we'd talk an' I'd listen. An' then Anna would come, maybe. She was younger but taller, blonde-haired. Good-looking kid. She really liked me, believe it or believe it not. Way she looked at me. Sometimes Gerry'd get jealous, angry. I just said fuck you she's my friend too if it's a problem for you then tough shit.

Sometimes go on a school trip someplace, maybe nature trip, I don't know, something. By some river lookin' at flora, fauna. Whatever. I remember some beetle or someth'n' walkin' on the water. By a riverbank, shaded under trees. Everyone had a box lunch 'cept me. Sat apart by an old tree, everyone on blankets by the river, nobody looked my way. Gerry said fuck them. He'd shove their fuckin' faces under the water, hold them there, see the bubbles, eyes popping, scratching their fingers on the rocks. A teacher brought me an apple, some chips. Askin' questions. I just chewed the apple. Gerry used to catch things. Animals, birds, fish, frogs. Anythin'. Skin the fish, gut them, kill rabbits. Do stuff to them. Times she told me fold the goddamn clothes, screamin' an' stuff, I'd go down the riverbank with Gerry. Anna? What about Anna? Why do I fucking bother with you. Rank deceiver, fantasist, preening jay. Jelly-bellied, roll-over recidivist. The stench of your heavy, sweating coat, preposterous hat pulled down. Beyond. Without. Outside.

Gerry, wild, hair red, dirty, wide, hungry lips, loose, apart, lolling, careening, tongue hanging, small, hard eyes darting. Hands large and boney, black like he'd been scrabbling for scraps of coal. Said rabbit meat was fine uncooked. Same as pork, squirrel, chicken, cat, I mean taste different, all taste good raw jus' the same. Taste kinda dry when cooked, takes some of the flavour out. Feelin' your teeth slide off the bone. Firm, somethin' to chew, smell of raw flesh. Kept his nails long for tearin' things up. Dirty, broken, used the nails get a grip on somethin', tear it apart. Sometimes his teeth. Teeth like some fuckin' animal, two big yellow canines either side of his mouth. Take a hold with his teeth an' tear at it, tearin' it apart like some fuckin' dog, shakin' his head. Slidin' roun' 'n the mud on all fours jus' like some animal, tryin' to get a hold of somethin', usually fish. Caught a squirrel once - fuck knows how. Shot it maybe. Hidin' just roun' side of some tree. Never saw the fuckin' squirrel, then he's got this thing in his hands, big, strong hands, claws with them nails, swingin' it by the tail, usin' his teeth. Don't remember any shot. Can't have just grabbed this thing. I don't know. Maybe. Gerry did 'bout anythin'.

One time climbed a tree, went out along a branch, somehow got his feet tight in some place, somewhere coupla branches split off different ways, hung there upside down, hangin' by his feet, legs, like some fuckin' bat, wavin' his arms, shoutin', screechin' like some fuckin' weird bird, somethin'. Broke his fuckin' neck if he'd dropped on his head. Pulled himself up, like one a them insects, twistin' its body back aroun'. Weirdest thing I ever seen. Sometimes Anna was there, check shirt, jeans, blonde hair. Standin' watchin', or pokin' somethin' in the river. One or other, both maybe, start some weird baby talk. Some weird stuff, Dadda-dadda-dadda, where you do day dadda, do in dar dadda. Some crazy shit. Runnin' by the river screechin' like crazy birds, flappin' their arms about, like hens had their heads pulled off, throwin' stones, rocks at the fish. All that kind of stuff. Couldn't stop them doin' the crazy stuff. Once it started, once the mood started that was it. Period.

The Investigation

We shall disdain yet not ignore this treachery. Go out. Go out among them and seek out their ways. Listen for their secret voices. Alluding, allusion, indirect perhaps, implying, implicating, deceiving, deceit. Gross treachery. Place your ears to the walls of their bedchambers. Listen for their noisome voices. Hear the lies, contumacies amid the noxious moans. Trace your footsteps closely within theirs. They turn left, be it first, second, third and so on, so do you turn left, first, second, third, as it may be. Right, first, second, third, fourth and so on, do you follow in like method. Mimicking their movements, caressing the air, assumed stillness, silence, waiting. Coiled, still. Calculating distance, speed, movement, direction, left, right, as it may be and so on. Movement. Pressing, imperceptible. Closing, hidden, concealed, concealing shadows beside the silver spike-topped railings.

Watch, watching, observing for their secret vices. Therefore set watchers at points of ingress and egress. Dark-garbed watchers, heavily-coated, sweating, wide-brimmed hats pulled down, concealing, concealed muzzles, masks, dark shadows of scabrous stubble, glazed eyes watchful, watching. Then other watchers, listeners, sifters, collators, cross-referencers and so on, with assumed stillness, silent, alert for obscure spaces, secrets, concealed hides in attic spaces perhaps, some hidden trapdoors, secret locks, concealed, forbidden entry-points. Some secret spaces, above bedchambers, as it may be, above the scenes of flagrant writhings, loathsome lascivious fornications, amid discarded lumber. Rocking horses, leaning, tilting as may be from broken rockers, eyes gouged, bodies discoloured, legs distorted. Sweet, rancid breath of decay like some mud-dragged blanket lying over all these places. Reluctant breath of sunlight, tainted, halting, settling at last on cluttered floor. Clear some space. Place your ears to the floor above their bedchambers. Learn their hidden secrets. Let the evidence then be gathered, sifted, collated and so on.

Every Day I Die

I never spoke to them, they never spoke to me. Get that through your thick skull. Never seen her face before. Period. Everything is confusion. Is. What is. I remember nothing except that everything is chaos. My life is chaos. My life is death in slow motion. Every day I die, wake again, have to face another day of remembering. I remember nothing. I was never there, not ever. Never saw any of these people in my life. No good shoving that in my face, pal. You - you put me through this, all your stinking lies and fabrications. Stink. The stench of your sweating, flabby body, scabrous sagging flesh, bumptious tilting beard, wag wag a-wagging, folds of repulsive drooping tissue, fold, folding. Ululating voices, crying, wailing in my head. The beating of the drum. The heat. Sweating.

Watching

Pumpin' gas. I met her. So she was there. What did you do. Watching, watchfulness. Let us say observing. Observance. Your rituals. Swill your dirty maw with stinking wash. Scrape those crooked tombstone teeth. Arm yourself at every point with flagrant fabrications. Each every one heard a thousand times before. Endless rehearsal. Rehearsed to the point of nausea. Invoke your mother. Bring her into this, why not. Soil the gilded image, pollute her memory. Drag your pitiful recollections through the mire. Her eye, lightly-lifted lip, arm raised. Reliable indicators indeed, were the indications themselves reliable. Check the oil, check the tires, fill the gas. Cracked sidewall, loose hose, leakin' oil. Oil leakin' from the sump, maybe the filter. Something. So she was there. Pumpin' gas. Four dollars fifty an hour I paid. After a couple of weeks she left. Didn't like the work. Something. Names. I don't remember any names. I never had any intentions.

Interactions? I wasn't there. But don't think I didn't notice. I saw the way you carried yourself. That heavy, shuffling gait. Grey stubble. Eyes darting. I concentrated on the job in hand. Check the oil, tires, fill the gas. Sure it was hot. Wipin' the sweat, the stink of gas. The dust would cover the pumps. I'd get a bucket, hot water, sponge. So she'd serve the gas while I cleaned the pumps. Steam rising from the water, heat on my hand from the water, the foamy, cleansing liquid, the face of the pumps clean, clear after I wiped the dust. Dried them off with a cloth. Didn't want to leave them wet even in that heat. Didn't want streaks on the glass. Watching. Watchfulness. Let us say observing. Dials showed the gallons, dollars. Stink of the gas, diesel. I tipped the dirty water in the dust. Watched it soak into the dust. Becoming part of the dust. A slight stain, outline. The heat. Tied her hair up in a ponytail, out of the way of serving the gas. Checked shirt, small checks of red and white. Golden blonde hair tied up. Blue jeans. She took off so I had to get someone else. I wasn't mad. These things happen.

The Riverbank

Talking, arguing, disputing. Let us say. Brown hair down her back, eyebrows heavy on her pocked face, like some animal, squirrel, rat, hands fiddling with stuff, bag, purse, whatever, sitting back, legs stretched out. Pink jacket, on the back some silver material, Pretty Miss, Missy, whatever. Never stopped talking, teeth, uneven, yellow, flying here, there, yapping, I said this, he said that, I said that, he said this. Boyfriend in some place fifteen miles north. Must have been some ugly fuck. Usual stuff, some argument 'bout nothin', she said, told him where to shove the fuck off, told her to get the fuck out, stuff throwed around, hands raised. Parked off the road, walked aways through the trees, nobody around, still talking, riverbank area deserted. River was high, moving fast. Dark. We stayed a while, did the usual stuff. Then the accusations, accusing. Screaming her head off. Usual stuff. I wasn't listening by this time.

The Invitation

She was across the street. It was a hot morning. Shimmering, shimmying, swaying, swirling. Hair like the hot, driven sands, golden, gilded. So it was hot. Sashaying, gliding. Golden head stuck beneath the hood. I pulled up. An electrical fault, maybe. Maybe I was already there. Watched, watching. She looked up, saw me, smiled. Oh yes it was she who smiled. The invitation, unspoken promise. Better if I stayed within my vehicle. Remain within your vehicle. Hands on the wheel. Better that I stayed. Looked. Looking at. But my intention was clear, I would remain within the vehicle. Whatever the provocation, no matter what form of words or lascivious manipulations I would remain firm. Hands on the wheel, remain within your vehicle. The heat. The sweat was in my shirt, hot and cold. The parking lot was deserted, just me within my vehicle. But she was golden, gilded, eyes of greeny-blue, beckoning. I remained within my vehicle. The heat through the windshield, the glare. I wound my window down three inches, maybe four. Let us say four. My hands remained on the wheel. I looked straight ahead through the windshield. I no longer moved my head, kept my head still, looking straight ahead through the windshield. The glare. And I knew then winding down my window was a mistake. I continued to remain within my vehicle, looking straight ahead but the opened window was a mistake, it betrayed me. Was there cooling breeze calling through those four inches, perhaps there was. Still she was there across the parking lot. I remained within my vehicle looking straight ahead. My shirt was wet. Looking at. I told her it was an electrical fault. Ran my hands over the distributor, plug leads. Solenoid. Maybe the earthing cable. The battery was turning it. She smelled of summer flowers overlaid with sweat. Maybe the sweat was mine. The heat was bouncing off the windshield and chrome. The lot was dusty. The blue was sealing it in, tight, airtight. The heat was the moment, no before or after. So we went in my car to get my tools, tools of the trade. She played with the radio, some hip-hop, rap, whatever. Some shit. I got angry. Kept it in me, just the noise of it, the heat and glare. Stretched out her legs, blue jeans, long, slim. Muscles, sinews, blood vessels, internal organs. A wrapper, barely covering. Laughter like a musical box. But that damn noise was driving me crazy. Told me about her mother. Lived with her mother and younger sister, used to play out in her yard. Catching a ball, playing late in the evenings with her friends, crickets chirping, whatever, laughing in the growing darkness, the air now fresh, cool, fragrant. Fuck, that rap shit. Could have told her to turn it the fuck off, but wanted, trying to keep things cool. The riverbank, cooler now. Betrayed by three inches, maybe four, window wound down just that much. Wound, wending.

The Coverlet

There is no price. No release, no freedom. Crowding. The beating in my head, pounding. The riverbank. No, not riverbank. Nowhere. Wait. Wait. I remember soft coverlet. Cotton, say, soft silks. Let us say soft coverlet of silk, sheets, white muslin, sparkle white, scent, soft scent of soap, soft, gentle powders. Polished mahogany chest, was it mahogany, some lighter wood perhaps, chestnut let us say, deeply grained patterns of growth, seasons passed, passing, polished shining sheeny bright, fresh smell of polish, cut flowers too, let us say. And there upon the chest of drawers, smell of polish, yes, cut flowers, yes, the smell of one, the other, combining, merging, scent, odour of careful governance, restraint, order, neat, tidy as it may be. And on the chest, beneath the vase, sparkle vase half-filled with clearest water holding cut, sweet-perfumed flowers, between the two, protection for the polished textures, grains of chestnut chest, delicate, delicately-wrought ornamental filigree, no not filigree, more doily, not doily, let us say mat, lace mat, white, of intricate, decorative, ornamental form, ornamented, yes, yet functional too, protecting polished, textured grains of chestnut chest from sparkle vase half-filled with clearest water holding cut sweet-perfumed flowers. So now we have soft coverlet of cotton say, or silk. White coverlet, white muslin sheets, white ornamental mat of lace protecting chestnut chest, all white, all sparkle white. Cut flowers. Scent. What more. Curtains half-drawn. Curtains of bright flowers, red, ochre, blue, green stalks, leaves, twisting, intertwining. Soft, thick sunlight drifting through half-drawn curtains, drifting, falling with soft, sighing sigh upon the soft white coverlet. More. What more. Just this. Soft hand. Brush, brushing, caressing pure soft skin of chubby cheek, tiny brow, softest, lightest touch. Touch of silk, soft, caressed. Caressing. All lies.

Consolation

Let us say. Let us say in death, a condition you obviously fear, quite inexplicably in my view - your extinction occasion surely for - forgive me - universal and unreserved rejoicing. But which be that as it may - in death, I say, is not an instant just as infinitely long, or short, as infinity itself? Difference surely there is none. There is - now for it - no meaningful difference. Remember this, my friend, when you are called. Find comfort there. Consoling thought. Sweet consolation. There, if anywhere.

The Empty Lane 2

The empty lane. Have I not made it clear by now there was no lane. Why don't you fucking listen. Or even - or even if we so grant this postulate of lane, working hypothesis, whim, plaything, whatever, the lane was empty. Have I not in fact made this sufficiently clear. Your roving eye and scabrous beak, seeking carrion from ego's height, lighting on some supposed movement, some trick of shadow, flutter of leaves perhaps, casting phantom strollers, dark-coated, leisurely wanderers, faces turned, closed. Your keening eye, sifting, searching amid the lager cans, discarded sweet wrappers, assorted debris, last autumn's leaves, grit and so on, displaced ventilator cover, attuned to vacant flesh, swooping. Your jagged thoughts turning, keening, careening, to prey amid the sweet, bright flowers of the gorse, willows, fluffy catkins pushing through the tall silver spike-topped railings. Along the worn and dusty path, no tipping (by order), piles of bricks, concrete slabs, discarded fridges, brambles lasciviously arching upon themselves. Sudden scything whoosh of nearby train. Tik-tik-tik-chik-a-tik-a-wooing from topmost branch. Splitting bags of garbage. Bright yellow gorse. Droning bee. Moss. The rhythmic cooing of pigeons, overlapping in their coos, repeat, repeat, repeating.

The Truck Stop

You watch the way she moves. Taken with her movement, way of moving. Steps, stepping, striding. High-stepping motion, long-limbed striding. Hair like a fantail, frizzed, frizzy, long dark plumage rippling from the back of her head as she struts, strutting. Dark, darkish skin, white jacket, some shiny white material like leather, some hard, creased plastic, shining, catching glow of streetlight, hard glow of the streets. Dark jeans, black, pointed boots. Hands, fingers, freighted, bedecked with gold, ornaments, embellishments, trinkets, shining, reflecting, catching hard glow of streetlights, signs brightly lit, glare of headlights, swinging, passing. Turned in to some bar. Watching, catching sight from sink, pit, truck park. Talking with a bunch of guys. Truckers. Some truck stop, burgers, beer, loud games of pool, muffled clatter of voices, shouting. Brightly-lit uncurtained windows, laughing, wide-open maw, shiny, shining teeth, white, bright as narrow fan of light thrown out, deserted truck park, dark, hulking, shrouded forms. Usual shit, C&W, heavy rock, wailing voices, loose-tuned twanging, carried with the light, cutting up the dark sky, cloud, ragged scraps torn from larger fabric, forms. Glare of uncurtained windows catching in the windshield, smeared, smearing glare, dirt playing on the windshield.

Beards and denim. Loathsome combination. Beards, tattoos, worn, stained denim. Good ol' boys. Way we do it down south, boy. Settle things Tennessee-style. Beards, tattoos, denim. Beards bright-lit, beards dark-shadowed. You ask me why I dwell on beards, why I place them so obviously in the spotlight, fanlight and so on. Why I throw this bright, searching gaze upon them, as if in, or within, all answers lie. You think, doubtless, of your own unholy outcrop, loathsome greying stubble, masquerading muzzle of some ravening beast. Bestial. No doubt. An understandable inference, common factor and so on. Howsoever. The door swung open, slanting, tilting rhomboid etched for a moment in the black sink truck park. Two truckers, bearded, striding, rambling, splitting respective ways to respective vehicles, cabs, narrow bunks concealed within hulking, shrouded forms.

Window wound down a precise distance or amount, let us say amount, be it three, four, five inches perhaps. I have not encountered the postulate of five before now, fresh evidence perhaps, unexplored avenue. As it may be. The engine, fired, low muffled roar from under the hood. I pulled up. Striding, swinging, stark definition, defining glare of headlights. Her face at the window, wide-boned, dark-hued skull, wide-spaced eyes, five inches, five, yes, let us say five perhaps, hardly more. Beer on her breath, sheer, stark whiteness of her teeth. Invitation, response, counter-invitation, let us say proposal, proposition. My intention clear. There was never betrayal of my intentions. They remain, remained clearly defined. Stretched out her legs, dark, pointed boots. Cruised the district a while, stopped at some all-night store. She bought a six-pack, candies, milk. Put the bags next her legs down the footwell. Smell of cheap perfume, sweat. Mine, perhaps. Said she had no particular plans. Then of course I wonder, for the night, following day? Lives with a friend, she said, stopping over a week, maybe two. Hence the milk, I guessed. Speculation, but my thoughts were not centred exclusively on her milk, or reason for buying it. My thoughts, such as they were, neutral, cold, abstract, containing no intentions or overt motivations beyond control over my immediate environment, questions of right, left, fast, faster, slow. Stop. My emotions unimportant. We shall not discuss the matter of emotions, motivations, imperatives, unconditional moral principles, the unconditionality central to the imperative. You claim the Grand Design defence? You repudiate free will? I was not referring to the Design Argument, far from it. Sluggish senses blind to the inherent paradox. So be it.

Said she'd be movin' on in a week, maybe two. Had to make a little money, she said, get the bus fare. Same old. Had a daughter, eight years old. Up in Springfield. Adopted when she was a baby. Seen her three times. Last time didn't want to know. Started crying. Only got one photo. Five years old, hair in pigtails. I kept it in me, the noise of it, pounding in my head, heavy beating of the drum. Usual shit, playing with my head, trying to play with my emotions. She got a tissue from the pocket of the white jacket. We parked next to an empty playground, mesh fencing, scatter of rubbish, broken glass. I cut the engine. Turned off the lights. Dark. Void. Empty.

Peace

Lazy movement of the water. Torpid. In the shallows horizontal ripples, merging, meshing with their own shadows, weaving, waving. Dead stalks of reed grass, almost white, pushed down. Worn, cracked ground. Compacted mud, trodden, friable, dusty surface. Decomposing plastic bags fluttering gently. Simple wooden bridge, lichen, decayed, decaying, grey moss either side of narrow footway. Imperceptible breath touching, breathing, brushing surface of sunlit pool. Dead trees casting dark mesh, complex lattice, superimposed on play of light and shade. Deep layers of mud, decaying matter, sunlight, lit, revealed, hidden. Light, shade. Peace, stillness.

Darkness

Pushing through dark, half-drawn curtains. More curtains beyond. Darkness. Was the darkness of the curtains, or some other darkness beyond. Was there a beyond. Or simply more half-drawn curtains, dark, darker, as it may be. Not daring to approach, approaching notwithstanding. A hand appears, reaches out. Was the hand mine, or of my own making, that is a conscious or, should I say, subconscious yet still willful invention. A hand that could have belonged to anybody perhaps, yet was mine in the sense - and perhaps only in this sense - of being the fruit and outcome of my willful yet subconscious deliberation.

Let us define the darkness, its quality, degree, texture and so on. That it was dark, that much is clear. So we shall say dark, darksome. Emitting, reflecting, let us say transmitting no light. Or, rather, let us qualify the statement. No suggesting absolute, unconditional, categorical, as it may be, which all available evidence, collated and so on, may not substantiate. So we shall qualify, modify, let us say moderate the statement. Little. Let us say little. Who, you will say, am I to utter absolutes, as it may be no, empty, void and so on. To affirm, make affirmation, let us say assertion. You, from lofty watchtower of self-esteem, high, remote, shining ashlar tower, gazing portentously above circular colonnade, or rather balustrade, white, radiant, creamy-white stone, newly-dressed, clean-hewn. Limestone perhaps. The setting appropriate to great metaphysician of tainted dreams, seer, prophet, staring blindly into nothingness. The infinity of ignorance, long, darkling shadows of diseased imaginings.

Is darkness subject or subject predicative (darkness was there: there was darkness). So many questions to be answered, revealed, evidence uncovered, collated, cross-referenced, pertaining as it may be and so on. Is the darkness subject, in and of itself, the quality, nature of the darkness being definition in and of itself, that is, in reflecting, emitting, transmitting little or no light. Doubt remaining in the absence of fresh evidence as to the degree or absolute absence of light, corollary to which (if proven) the degree or absolute nature of the darkness. Have half-drawn curtains been pushed aside in unseemly scrabble to define the nature of the darkness. False fruit, perhaps. Half-drawn curtains, parted, drawn farther, let us say pushed aside by half-seen hand, fruit and outcome of subconscious deliberation, revealing darkness beyond, darkness in and of itself, as it may be. Or yet more half-drawn curtains, more half-seen hands pushing, parting, or if not pushing, disturbing, lightly fluttering, rippling the darkling fabric, cotton, linen, whatever, of darksome half-drawn curtains. Hands, half-seen, curtains, receding infinitely into darkness beyond, without.

Lost. Entombed in darkness. Dense wood of predicates, verbs transitive, copulas and the like, darkish, darkling. Let us say be, seem, tastes, because, are, is and so on. As may be. May. Subjunctive use in this instance. Hardly. Merely component of rhetorical device, expression, let us say phrase. Period. Technicalities beyond your narrow range, above, beyond. Twitching beard, jaunty, scabrous tilt, jutting, beyond, across, overhanging smooth white parapet of high, white, shining watchtower. Circular, balustraded. Sightless gaze into void beyond. Darkness.

Bird of Paradise

I renounce and repudiate everything I have said up to this point. I reject and repudiate all previous statements. There was a degree of coercion. Let us say degree. Coerce. Coerciveness. Let us say force. Brute hand, raised. Lip lifted. If not then the usual tricks. The sleight of hand, the friendly glance, betray. Betraying. You seek to confound me with your verbal tricks. You fence, you joust, aim your halberd at my chest, rank deceiver. Plumed bird of paradise, bright feathers spread, displaying. Let us say display. Rank plumage. Bumptious tilt. Oh, then if not force, certainly the usual tricks. The hidden snare, loop, looping. Entangling. Ensnaring. Let us say. You dare cross words with me? I who have won first prize for gymnastics, been awarded gold medal for my *pas de deux*, though dancing often alone. Awarded moreover in stately ceremony, dark-coated prize giver, solemn downturned chin, dress coat, black shoes carefully placed, planted, perfectly in line, shined, a slight tilt from the hips, bowed, bowing, the chin downturned, the gaze far from meeting my own, turned always to my chest. Dark, tall, straight figure slightly, partially tilted. Clean shaven, the hair dark, shiny, carefully arranged, a suggestion of pomade. The contrast could hardly be more pronounced. That bumptious tilt, the greyed and greying strands, rank stubble, lank, flabby, flesh-hung wattle. Brightly-coloured bird of paradise, preening flea-ridden plumage in all the grandeur of your folly and pretension. Flabby, flea-ridden muddle. Beyond. Outside. Without. Remaining at all times within my vehicle. Disdaining the invitation, enticement, entrapment. Beckoning. Watching.

The Darkling Sky

Darksome sky, now darkly frowning. Continuous line of houses, contiguous. Descending. Repeated motifs. The repetition. Window, windows, staring, blinded as it may be, doors, boarded, closed, blinded, repeat, repeated, endless repetition. Heavy-coated passers-by, faces averted. Dark, heavy, dragging garb. Sweating, as may be, despite the seeping rain from darkling sky. Bedraggled couple, dragging feet, defeated rain-smeared faces. Clutching bags of booze, crisps, tabs. Tired, discoloured clothes. Trainers dragging, trailing. Sour sidelong look, antagonistic questioning, stabbing glance, then resolutely turned, turn, turning back of empty faces. A cat, hunched, scuttling warily, cautiously, glancing nervously, crossing the glistening road towards some empty littered lane. Noise of a can rolling endlessly, descending, falling. Rain, gushing, forcing endless rattle from the empty can, trapped, empty resonance. Repeated emblems, motifs. Roofs, glistening, dipping, diminishing with gentle descent of perspective. Repeat, repeating. Dipping, glistening, descending.

Brief, febrile flickering of consciousness, pressed between two infinities. The furies of sensation, driving on to point of intoxication. Gripping, driving. The unaccountable pressing drives, pounding, pressing, beating. Screaming. The scything, knife-edged scream in the abyss. Tall, blonde, fifteen years old, as may be. Straw-blonde hair glistening, damp fabric of coat, jeans. Caught in squally gust, flinching before the onslaught. Bag of groceries split, splitting, spilt among the random litter, grass, weeds sprouting from cracked concrete, asphalt. Spreading. From some half-drawn curtain a hand, raised. Beyond. Darkness.

The Riverbank 2

The riverbank. Fast flowing, potent in the dimming evening haze. The water rushing, pounding in my ears, my head singing. The light dimmed, dimming. Spread herself on the grass by the riverbank. Spread, spreading. Revealed. Left some guy in Nashville, she said. Bright suit, pointed shoes, sharp in his manner, direct. Some bozo, I thought, two a dime, enough to play on her. Maybe not the sharpest tool in the box. Drawling her way through some tale. Promised her money, didn't say what for. Same old, I guessed. Promised her money, then cut up rough when she made demands. Legitimate, she said. What she was owed, she said. Hundred dollars, maybe hundred fifty. Smilin' through his teeth at her, hand raised. She said. Her voice cutting rough across and through the river, my head ringing. Pounding of the river, the water rushing, pounding. Dark clouds above chasing the moon. Sweating. Overcoat stinking of damp rank sweat despite the coolness of the evening. Trees, turning black now, looking down, watching, observing. Still her mouthing maw, and now my heart ringing in my chest, in my head, nothing I could do. Screaming, the look in the eye. Poised. Stillness. My head still pounding. Rushing of the river, dark, potent.

The Moaning of the Pumps

Heat, dust. The moaning of the pumps, the whirring of the dials. Try to focus on the job in hand. Don't spill the gas on the paintwork. Sixteen dollars. Sure, checked the oil, hoses, tires. Coolant's a tad on the low side, sidewall's cracked, left rear. Sure, no problem. Take care, now. Wind picked up the dust, died, settled, warm touch of breeze. Sweating. Focus on the job. Always in the corner of my eye. Good worker. Blonde hair like shiny metal in that sun. I said to her do you use sun block, need to protect your skin this weather. She said sure, smiled, tilt of her head. Inviting. I was concerned, protective. Sure was hot. The heat was startin' to pound in my head. Boom, boom, boom. Got some water, foamy, cleansing liquid, washed the pumps while she served the gas. Smell of the gas. Couldn't shut her out. Always in the corner of my eye.

The Box of Secrets

I was never there. Not ever. Period. Don't put words in my mouth, fuck-face. Forgive me. Let me tell you why, the why of which, that is relating to which, the question of that being that I was never there. The absence, its unconditional nature. In that nothing was there. I include myself in this nothing, nothingness. I exclude nothing. Well you may wonder, ponder perhaps. Vacancy. Void. I am, that is the am I was, am perhaps, was part of this. Wait. The evidence may yet become clear, water-tight, largely uncontaminated. Committed in, within, my box of secrets. Oh you would love access to this. You already see, in that characteristic glittering covetousness, the key, shining, shining. Your very breath grows heavy. Large, elaborate steel instrument, may it be, decorative embellishment in the bow, or head, call it bow, let us say bow, that part, the part being at the far end, away from stepped configuration designed to throw tumblers, turned, turning, let us say jugglers, acrobats, minstrels, mute in mournful consolations. Your sour breath, quick panting breath now breathing over glittering key. So now you have the answer perhaps. Spreading, now pounding. Inserting, forceful, forced insertion, weighing now heavy within reluctant lock, heart beating, pounding in diseased cavity, carcass, noisome carapace. Foul fluids, contaminants, infecting the very air. Everywhere stench of decay. Stink. The turning of the lock, cold, hard instrument, turning, turned, greased by your foul presence. The box of secrets. The lifting of the lid. Revealed, revealing.

Out of True

Tilt. Inclination, out of true. What is true. Let us say true. Even the Earth is tilted, so it is said, is that not then true. Then is nothing true. I ask only out of academic interest, it is of little significance to me personally. The tilt, or not, as it may be, of an object, as ephemeral to me as your loathsome, flabby body. Forgive me. The bumptious high-strutting tilt of your beard. You feel the word has subconscious significance. If so from which beginner's guide did this profound insight spring. Attack, overthrow in tilt or joust. Take care you don't tilt too far and thereby fall into an abyss of your own making. Each thought marked, measured, labelled. Encircling darkness. Tilting, turning. Turning point. Point of no return, beyond, without. Oh, but I see you require some necessary nourishment. Go ahead. Greedy hands, picking, stuffing, eyes darting. An animal at bay, dragging the carcass to some dark corner, eyes boring, lip lifted, dismembering the carcass with savage tilt of neck, twisting, pulling, the deep, dark red of the blood, white stringy sinews, thick fibrous meat. Your narrative sickens me. Oh, forgive me.

The Turning

Despite invitation, enticement, enticing, I turned away. Turn, turning. The empty lane. I purposely avoided the empty lane. I would take a long detour, through crowded streets, market stalls, clustered groups with hostile, mocking faces, simply to avoid the empty lane. A selfless stratagem. Scorning faces, insulting, deriding. A bearded vendor, market stall proprietor, small, bearded, I mean in terms of stature, hopping, hobbling with surprising speed, streaming insults, hopping alongside, crabbing with surprising speed, dripping invective, spittle flying, coating dark and noisome beard. Cold pebble eyes filled with coarse intent, hopping, gesticulating, arms windmilling furiously across my face and person. Of course I turned, turning that is as far as was possible, my neck turned, keening, careening, ignoring, deriding in my turn, as it may be, though not openly, not overtly, not in any sense with demonstrative intent or indeed effect. At least that was my avowed intention, affirmation, avowal, that is to myself. As it were a contract between myself, that is my conscience, moral dimension and so on, if that is my self, and my will to have what my ego considers that which is available, waiting, willing for me to take. An act of gross egotism in itself, perhaps, to consider this moral dimension to be my true self, when some (many perhaps) would affirm my true self to be the ravening id untempered, that is unmoderated, let us say unmediated, by ego, superego and so forth. Forgive me. I stray into abstractions blessed by self-analytical powers lying many distant horizons beyond your feeble reasoning. Less than gracious gesture, perhaps. The guest invited to the feast left festering in anteroom, clad in dark, heavy overcoat, close, sweating perhaps, as it might be, wide-brimmed hat pulled down to, almost obscuring, eclipsing, loathsome stubble.

Then there is the matter of the turning. I turned, yes, that much is clear, undeniable, incontrovertible, confirmed by all available evidence, all known databases, cross-referencing and so on. So that much is clear. Very good. At last we stand on firm, clear ground with a view or views in all directions, even to distant horizons. Howsoever, the direction of the view, or views, analogous to the turning, my neck turned, keening, careening, as stated, the evidence clearly annotated, collated, cross-referenced and so on. As in the empty railway carriage, or wagon let us say, it is clearly established by all available evidence, databases and so forth, that the leaning, that is the direction of the leaning, or leaning out, as it may be, was to the left. What significance this is or is to the present case. How far can the device of analogy be employed, or deployed, in the present case to spread light on the direction of turning. Spreading. That I was turning, had turned, that I turned, yes, that much is clear, undeniable, incontrovertible. Let us say water-tight. Also the degree of turning. That it was as far as possible. This brings us into fresh realms of speculation in the absence of available data. How far was it possible for my neck to turn. Was the degree, or extent, let us say amount of turn the same in both directions. Still we have failed to address the central point, that is the direction of turn. Was it, in fact, to, or away from. This may prove of signal, let us say decisive, importance. May.

Perfume

She was glad enough for the lift. I swung around, neck careening dangerously, checking through the side window as I swing, pulling alongside. Rain, raining. Steady. Smearing, squeaking, whirring of the wipers on the windshield. The thumping, lumpy, subduing rattle under the hood. Deserted roadway this time of evening. A few isolated dwellings sitting back from laurel hedge, white paling fences, withdrawing, refusing to be drawn. Steady slanting strips of rain, kicking up the dust, falling back into gathering pools of mud and grit. Stuck her long legs down the footwell, blue jeans stretched out, smiling a smile from the corner of her lips, glad to be out of the rain. Playing with the radio. Hair shining, dewy glistening with the rain. Smell of the wet fabric, damp cotton of her jeans, cheap perfume in her neck, hair, wrists. Some old song, wailing, mournful, wheeling, a woman's voice. Crying. The noise of it, pounding. Laughing. Said she had to be back by ten. Mud, stones, grit, washed by the rain, some sharp-edged pebble, sharp-faced edge catching the tire, right rear perhaps. Pulled off down some track in the trees. Rain drumming on the windshield, voice on the radio, squawking, hollering, left me, left alone with only something. Some shit. Told her I kept my tools in the trunk, tools of the trade. She said what trade, laughing. Smell of her perfume, one foot up on the dash, blue jeans, damp fabric. Cotton. Came and stood by the trunk as I got the tools. Raindrops, trickling, dripping down through the leaves. Thick rich smell of undergrowth. Decay, decaying. Bright gold of her hair. Smell of perfume in her skin. Inviting. Thick deep soil, leaves, vegetation.

Musical Box

Watch. Watching. I see you. That poisonous hulking form. Loathsome progenitor of half-wits, misfits, nitwits. Seed of the unloved and unlovable, high priest of the unwashed and unwashable. Scavenging sink dweller, cess rat, sinkhole vizier, sinkage consultant, fawning roll-over servant of the sink, bootlicking freeloader, freebooting ass-licker. Forgive me. My spleen is active today, spleeny, spleenish. Let us say spleenful. As are the other internal organs, heart, liver, lungs, kidneys, stomach and so on. The flesh itself, the skin, an organ. Let us say dermis, epidermis and so on, technical terms beyond your ken. Let us say cover, covering, muscles, sinews, blood vessels. A wrapper, barely covering. Uncovered. Like a musical box. The lid. The lifting of the lid. The moment of lifting, the uncovering, the pouring of the light into the darkness, the shedding of the darkness. Pivotal moment. Let us say pivotal. Cover, covered. Uncovered. Revealed, revealing. The emptiness. The rushing of the river.

Dust

Oh contumely, contumely. You insinuate, postulate, form false images and formulations, where templates there are none. Your desert mind a void sans springs. Arid as vacant horizons. As dust, the dust of dead flesh. Arid waste, wasteful. The wastefulness. Dust, all dust.

Printed in Great Britain
by Amazon